PUMPKIN HEADS!

Wendell Minor

THE BLUE SKY PRESS / AN IMPRINT OF SCHOLASTIC INC. / NEW YORK

October is here.
It's time to pick
a pumpkin!

On Halloween
every pumpkin
becomes
a pumpkin head.

Some are big.
Some are small.

Some may float high in the sky.

Some peek

from

windows.

And some go
for a hayride.

Some pumpkin heads pretend to be cowboys...

or

snowmen...

or

witches!

Some

pumpkin heads

will greet

for trick-or-treat!

And

some will

scare crows.

Pumpkin heads
can be found
in the strangest
places.

Βut no matter where
you may find them,
pumpkin heads
of all shapes and sizes…

hope you have a

HAPPY HALLOWEEN!

THE BLUE SKY PRESS

Library of Congress catalog card number: 99-086364
ISBN 0-590-52105-5
10 9 8 7 6 5 4 3 2   0/0 01 02 03
Printed in Mexico   49
First printing, September 2000